This Little Piggy's Book of Manners

by Kathryn Madeline Allen
illustrated by Nancy Wolff

Henry Holt and Company · New York

Henry Holt and Company, LLC
115 West 18th Street
New York, New York 10011
www.henryholt.com

Henry Holt is a registered trademark of Henry Holt and Company, LLC
Text copyright © 2003 by Kathryn Madeline Allen
Illustrations copyright © 2003 by Nancy Wolff
Hand lettering copyright © 2003 by Nancy Wolff
All rights reserved.
Distributed in Canada by H. B. Fenn and Company Ltd.

Library of Congress Cataloging-in-Publication Data
Allen, Kathryn Madeline.
This little piggy's book of manners / by Kathryn Madeline Allen ;
illustrated by Nancy Wolff.
Summary: Some little pigs remember their manners and others do not.
[1. Etiquette—Fiction. 2. Pigs—Fiction. 3. Stories in rhyme.]
I. Wolff, Nancy, ill. II. Title.
PZ8.3.A4188 Th 2003   [E]—dc21   2002010858

ISBN 0-8050-6769-8 / First Edition—2003
The artist used gouache on Canson paper to create
the illustrations for this book.
Printed in the United States of America on acid-free paper. ∞
10 9 8 7 6 5 4 3 2 1

THANKS

For Nicholas, Michael, and Christina, my three little piggies
—K.M.A.

For my family
—N.W.

You're welcome

closed his mouth while he ate.

This Little Piggy forgot.

This Little Piggy Shared all of her toys.

This Little Piggy Said, "MINE!"

This Little PiGGy
waited his turn.

This Little Piggy...

This Little Piggy Pouted.

This Little piggy...

Spoke kindly to others.

WhEN I YELL!!!

You. Who Are You Calling RudE?

I said,

NOW! LiSTEN!

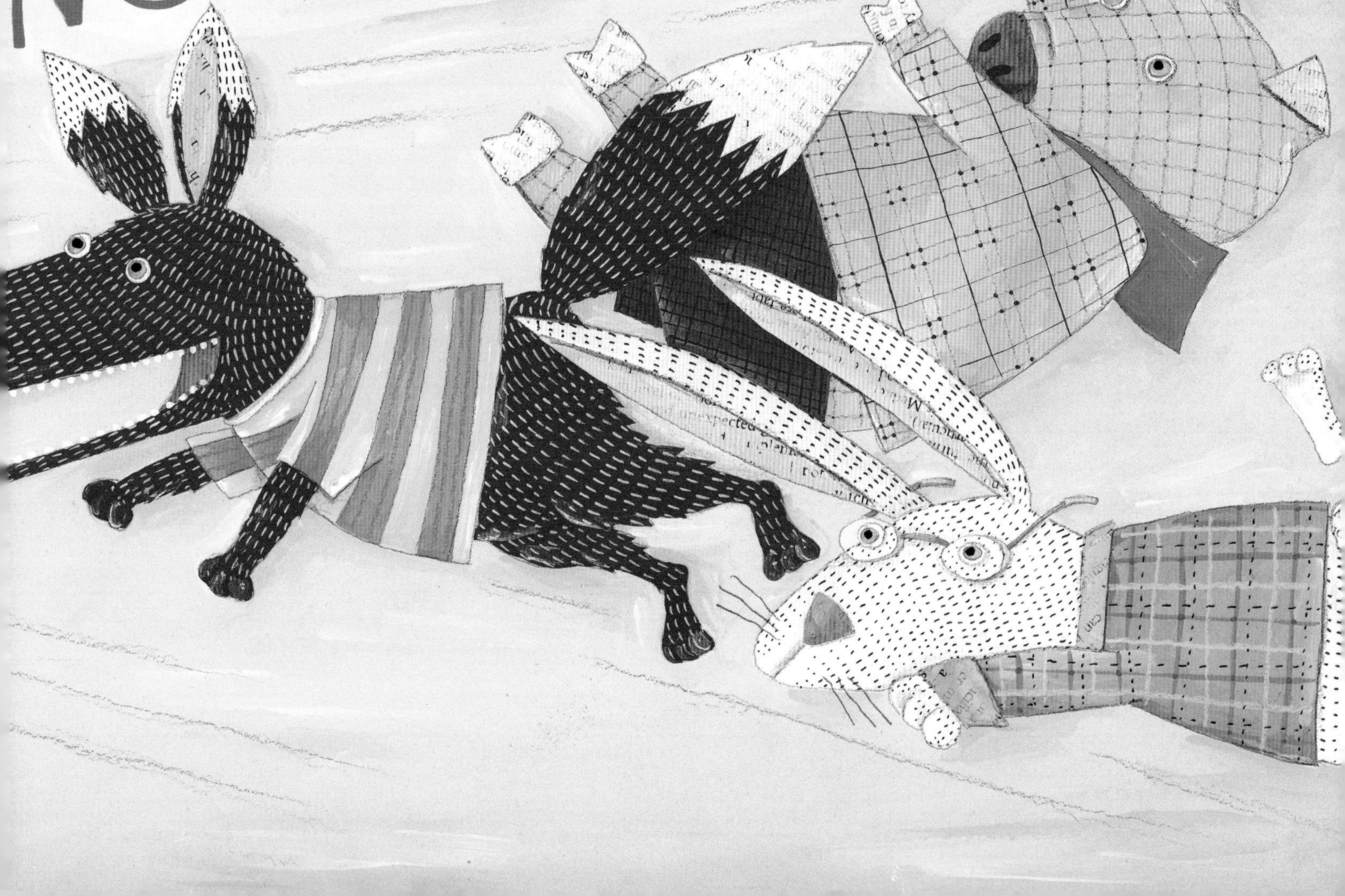

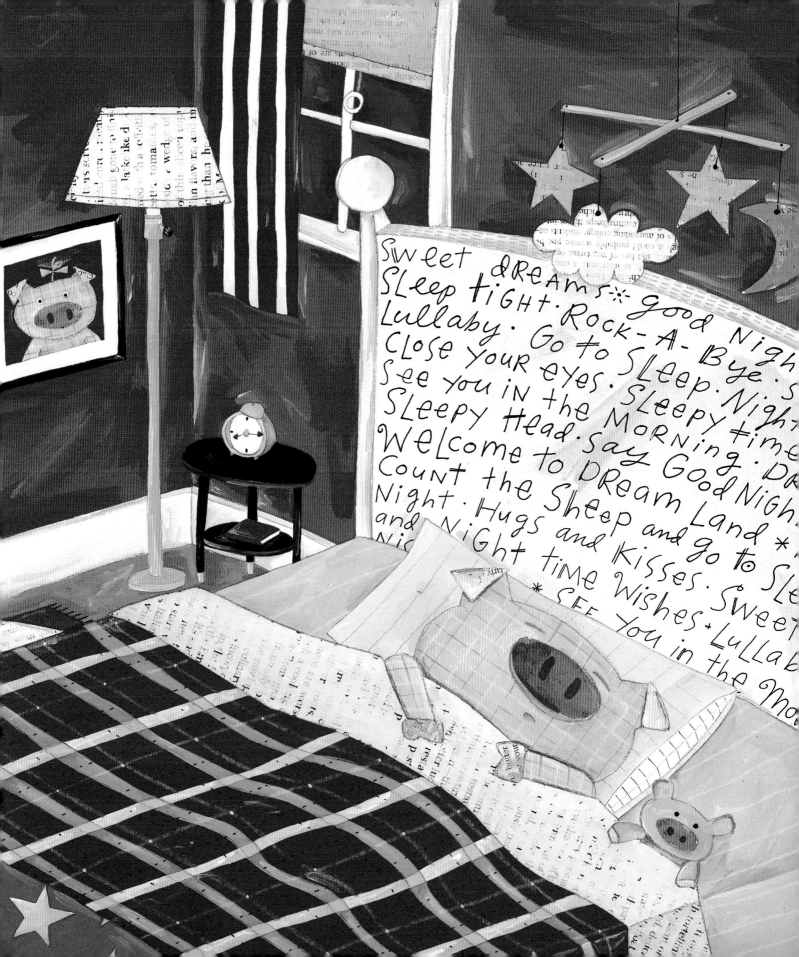

At times little Piggies

will practice their manners

(though sometimes they seem to forget them).

But if they remember,

the Piggies nearby

might say they are Pleased to have met them!